BLOOD FEATHER

This book is a work of fiction. The names, characters and events in this book are the products of the author's imagination or are used fictitiously. Any similarity to real persons living or dead is coincidental and not intended by the author.

The content associated with this book is the sole work and responsibility of the author. Gatekeeper Press had no involvement in the generation of this content.

Blood Feather

Published by Gatekeeper Press
7853 Gunn Hwy., Suite 209
Tampa, FL 33626
www.GatekeeperPress.com

Copyright © 2024 by Sarah Walker
All rights reserved. Neither this book, nor any parts within it may be sold or reproduced in any form or by any electronic or mechanical means, including information storage and retrieval systems, without permission in writing from the author. The only exception is by a reviewer, who may quote short excerpts in a review.

ISBN (paperback): 9781662952692
eISBN: 9781662952708

BLOOD FEATHER

Sarah Walker

Tampa, Florida

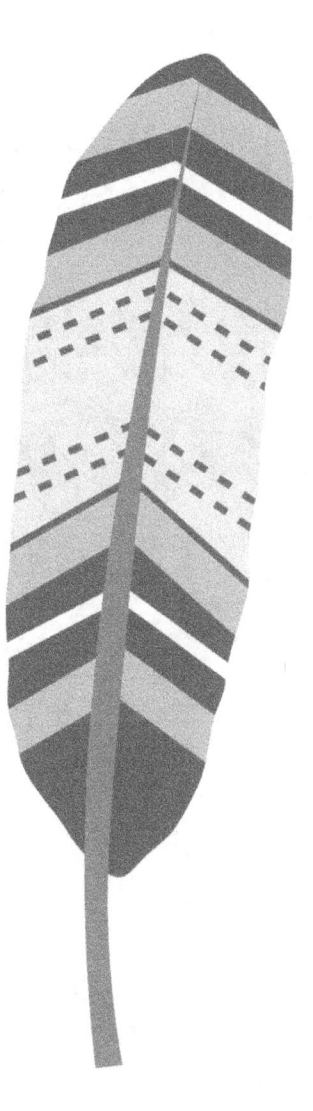

THE WITCHERY WAY

In 1878, forty Indigenous men were put to death for the crime of witchcraft in what is now known as the Shaman Slaughter of 1878. Of the forty, only Tyee managed to escape his fate by smearing his body with the blood of his slain brethren and concealing himself under the heap of the dead.

Once the blood ran cold, the Ditlihi set about the greedy process of robbing the bodies of their possessions. The deceased had donned sacred stones handmade into exquisite jewelry in preparation for what was to be the ultimate sacrifice to the netherworlds, payment to the A-sgi-na, as gifts from the damned. The Ditlihi tore away at the tribal artifacts, one by one, overloading their covetous pockets.

The clink of the copper-encrusted fluorite as it plummeted to the stained soil alerted the attention of Hiamovi, the high chief who ordered the bloodshed. Kneeling down to retrieve the fallen treasure, Hiamovi heard the gasp of desperation fleeing from the tangled stack of bodies. Angry, he jabbed his spear into the frames of the massacred. Suddenly, he felt a tug on his arm, and it was yanked clean from the elbow. Hiamovi slammed his free hand to the ground as a vicious force dragged him deeper into the carnage. Preoccupied with freeing himself, he failed to notice Tyee kneeling at his side. Tyee plunged a severed bone into Hiamovi's neck, sending the bone through his spinal cord, staking him to the earth. With

Hiamovi glued in place, Tyee spung from the butchery, chanting repeatedly as he fled, "A-sgi-na, A-sgi-na!"

The warriors readied themselves to tally the grim head count. Satisfied with the number, the dead were stretched out in ceremonial order while the putrid odor clung to their nostrils. A clap of thunder broke through the pink horizon, bringing forth a black rain that scorched the brawn of the Ditlihi. Their flesh slid to puddles at their feet. The melted skin married into the mud, collapsing the ground beneath the stance of each brave, pouring them into the cracks of the now blemished clay. The land stretched apart like deerskin from a hide, resealing after devouring the remnants of the executed, consecrating this soil to give birth to immoral transgression. Charred roots pushed up from the abyss, twiddling up to the forsaken Gods, holding tightly the spirits of the decimated Ditlihi, this Fatherland's properly stony heart. The last purities left were the embers that scattered wildly with the sweep of wind. Absent from the heavens were the celestial bodies, the candescent moon. Only ash from the dying fires sailed through the blackness. Cockcrow brought perturbation as the malevolent specter hovered over the Hialeah.

THE BLACK DEATH

When the Ditlihi failed to return by the rise of the following tawa, the Udalii sang prayers for the misplaced warriors to the heavens, fearing they'd never look upon the faces of their braves. At the command of Nizhoni, Udalii to Hiamovi, a Naalzheehi was assigned to retrieve the bodies of the Ditlihi. Cutting across the battlefield, the Naalzheehi sensed the dread that befell this once flourishing soil. The telltale symptoms of an ill wasteland, contaminated by sorcery, polluted by necromancy, devoid of bodies. Whatever lingered now would not be snaffled.

Melancholy, Naalzheehi brought empty hands with no justification to the Udalii. Dejection permeated the aura harboring the women as they yielded to the laws of the Manitou that sentenced their Ditlihi to meander the isolated in between the living and the dead. Nizhoni's form crumpled from the mass of despair worn across her shoulders. Tears cascaded down her cheeks, sending her emotions to unveil her ordained trajectory. Clutching the red clay in her fists, Nizhoni slathered the muddied soil across her face, concealing her virtue. She shook as she ordered the Naalzheehi: "Take me to the battlefront." In spite of his consciousness of the wicked that now inhabited the region, the Naalzheehi complied.

"Myths compressed with truths told around the bonfires kept me curious to his existence while apprehension restrained me from gallivanting. To many, this is the final chapter in their book of life. A place to rest the bones when the soul exits. Tonight, it's my redemption, disguised as sin. I've merely heard of the A-sgi-na; tonight, I ascertain him," Nizhoni said.

Agitation froze Naalzheehi's steed as it breached the threshold of the atrocious. Ascending from the frightened animal, Nizhoni unsheathed the Naalzheehi's macahuitl, hastily advancing past the safety of his reach. "Teach me suffering," she pleaded to Pawnee as she thrust the obsidian blade cavernous to her chest. Her torso folded, skimming the remainder of blade that failed to penetrate, revealing the future predestined her. The frenzied quake of the earth propelled the Naalzheehi to his back as the savagery of the Netherworld consumed Nizhoni's corpse. Trepidation brought him to his feet, and he hurtled to his horse, riding nimble, narrowly cheating the blackened fingers that stretched from the hungry abyss.

The imprecation outstretched to the tribe, ignorant to the devastation stampeding to the fore. The Udalii, clad in lamentation, dubiously prepared the last rituals for their Ditlihi. Assembling the leftovers of the tribe, infants and children in tow, they marched to the Mni. As they cornered the bend, a stranger sat stoic, elegant, on her stallion. Her ravishing beauty duped their cautious instincts of engagement as the Udalii never questioned her origins. Her hair was black as night, absent a moon, while her eyes protruded illuminance. Exquisite lips separated, bellowing out the sweetest of symphonies, hollowing the ears of her audience, clandestinely bewitching their intellect. Intimately mesmerized, the Udalii shepherded their offspring to the Mni. In succession, the Udalii involuntarily immersed each child's head in the water. It engulfed their tiny bodies, sending them to buoy above the surface. Instantaneously, the Udalii arose from the incantation to gaze about the horrors committed by their hands. Unpredicted, the Udalii's souls were wrenched from their skeletal exterior. As the ceremonial robes combusted, their bones disintegrated to ash.

Rapid transmogrification of the enchantress unmasked the Mephistophelian Skudakumooch. Her skin decomposed, and grotesquely festering spores discharged an otherworldly septicemia. Her veins were tethered to crevices of cleaved bone, and through the dark tresses that encased her erstwhile artistic features loomed her ghastly countenance. In uniform, her majestic creature reprised his nefarious skin, outlining the scolding lashes of the underworld. Flames snorted from his nostrils as he cantered into the shadows, the Skudakumooch at his side.

The Naalzheehi, belatedly to avert, caught sight of the bloated papooses sailing the Mni. He kneeled leaden to the reeds, dejected. The cloudburst transpired in sync with the wailing. "Cries?" pondered a bewildered Naalzheehi, as the lands were deserted.

Furtively, the Naalzheehi peeked through the reeds for the visage that complemented the doleful wailing. Merged with the outer dead tissue of the bark, crestfallen eyes surfaced, liberating streams of torment. "Ahanu, my child," uttered a friable voice. Staggered, the Naalzheehi gripped the rigid handle of his knife, probing the vicinity for its genesis. Openmouthed to his discovery, he peered into the ocular cranny. The frail voice apprised the Naalzheehi of the ungodly affairs that encompass his quintessence and that of the other within the inanimate trees. The Udalii penalized the children for bearing poundage to them as fatherless, provoking the resurrection of cannibalistic Paakniwat. Such a sacrilegious gesture warranted the epitome of barbarous damnation as the Udalii were condemned to peregrinate as Tah-tah-kle-ah. These fiendish stratagems were orchestrated by the Skudakumooch.

Harkening the chronicles, the Naalzheehi scrutinized his undertaking to Nizhoni in confidence. The acrimony tiptoed further to his intestines as he tried to swallow. The query was irrefutable: "What have I done?" he croaked. The breath of life interned, nucleus now of the timber, rebutted the Naalzheehi's culpability. Verklempt, the breath elongated his birchen bough, disseminating the infernal gospel. The A-sgi-na stitched up the falsehoods to procure Nizhoni for self-serving exigency, culminating the affliction.

As the spiel enumerated, the extant Ditlihi sprouted from the interiors of the thickets, blowing the gaff to their locus. The scenario painstakingly announced the veracity of the offspring, the treachery that befell the amenable benevolence of Nizhoni, unperceived. The Naalzheehi gave his undertaking to rectify the malfeasance. Unilaterally, he would hunt him. As he struck his left forearm, his ancestry adorned the weeping trees. The augmenting branches weaved concomitantly, achieving a circle of enchantment, armed with dinkum. "Take this, a testament of sorrow shall enfranchise her," petitioned the breath.

Five mothers impersonating cacodemon owls, the Tah-tah-kle-ah mythology publicized their malefic etiquette. These anathematized creatures clamored for Lex talionis gracing the Naalzheehi's side, his consultant coven in the realms of the netherworlds. A prerequisite to smite the Devil dictated a guileful dignitary, renounced from her loyalties, her quest for retributive justice chastened.

His feathered chaperones swarming the twilight, the Naalzheehi progressed into the witching hour. Hounding her footpath, the Naalzheehi beheld the spoors abandoned by her wretched stallion. Sulfur crisp, affixed to the ambience, the

Skudakumooch bordered the barriers of the apocalyptic. Demoniacal trickster, revamped at the crafts of the A-sgi-na, the Naalzheehi concedes her lore by referencing the admonition. Competent of assimilating beast or man essential for absolute domination of her rival. Vermilion orbs the omen to seek with qualms of confrontation.

Now more a mortal man, the Naalzheehi anticipates his adroitness. Stalking the grip of malodor in the arrokoth, the trills of his Tah-tah-kle-ah barked their forewarning to the Naalzheehi to the scatter of animal cadavers that fringed the terrain forth. Shrouded in the maikoh's carcass, one of many distinct variations, she scooched herself conveniently in the somber of the eclipse. Discreet, the Naalzheehi cuffed the ligneous shaft anchored rigid to the honed flint. Stiff in his grasp, he pounced prosperously to the nape of her snarled guard's hairs. Frantically, he wrangled her to submission, impelling his spear to her underbelly, extracting a hellish squeal from her vanquished incarnation. Unnerved, he purely retired the beast for the necromancer alchemized, unclothed, her beldam prevailed. Her decrepit fingers assailed for the Naalzheehi's throat, vigorously dissevering his head from the neck. The loyal Tah-tah-kle-ah ambushed, snaring her captive in the confines of the circle of enchantment. The entwined scion lacerated her pellicle, deep rooting her veins with the authenticity of her conception. The malefic firestorm was freed from her apertures as each perjury came forth, enkindling the terrain. The treen circle siphoned her bartered soul back to the netherworlds, shedding a solitary seared scarlet feather. The A-sgi-na's duplicity bared, the Skudakumooch yearned for her vengeance. A sanguinary rebellion loomed in the wake of her asseveration as her hex invigorated in the rise of Blood Feather.

She crawls to me. The grit of the road shreds the remaining flesh away from her raw knees. Her blood sizzles as it drops to the soil. The smell of her sweat produces a sickening aroma only one such as myself could find appetizing. Despite the sting of the earth that scrapes her wounds, she clings tighter, holding steadfast to her wall of agony. My tricks cloaked under my spoiled skin, I will present only the treats, for hers was the soul I've waited out mortality to embrace. Her shattered heart calls out to me as she drags herself to my salvation. With each passing inch, my cravings for her heighten. Drained of physical strength, she is in a weakened state of survival. A compromise of solace, deliverance lurks in the shadows of my deprivation. She asked me to gag the voices in her head, asphyxiate their bitterness that sours the end of her tongue. The force that channels her fuels my perversions as she begs. Grasping her neck, I oblige, delighted to assist her irrational state.

Sustained with a sweetness only her innocence could posses, my cravings are satiated. "Count down, clock, her beating heart. Secrets will spawn regrets, but words shall not slip past grey lips."

My purity interlaced his transgressions, summoning corruption with the clamp of his jaw. He held firm, swallowing the residue of my mortal life. "For your appetency, I render nourishment. I bestow you retribution."

The pain immeasurable, feverish, fulfills my aspirations masked in my belly. My blood ran red for the last time as I closed my eyes and sank my last breath deep into my lungs, exhaling to awake as vengeance.

Unbound from persecution, Tyee collapsed at the hush of the brook, releasing his contused head in the cool of the water, generating ripples that blurred his reflection as he sunk himself. The bite of his salt skimmed the rim of his lips, forcing them to crack wide open, spilling his cursed lineage into the crystalline river. Heavily, he hung in his own filth, bone weary from the melee. The wrinkles of the wave pushed towards him. He heard the singe hit the surface as the vapors lifted the sulfur to his open mouth. A-sgi-na stood statuesque before him, primed to collect the soul so morbidly vowed by Tyee. A-sgi-na's jaw unhinged from the decomposing tissue that time had encrusted to his skeleton.

"You betrayed me!" roared A-sgi-na. He advanced to the Adam's apple protruding plainly from Tyee's neck, slashing a single scratch, severing his head. Clasping at the mane attached, A-sgi-na carried his trophy off into the murk of the netherworld but not before decreeing malediction, punishment for the Shaman's scorn.

www.ingramcontent.com/pod-product-compliance
Lightning Source LLC
LaVergne TN
LVHW021750060526
838200LV00052B/3575